D1505618

# THE ZACK FILES

## Don't Count on Dracula

# LETTERS TO DAN GREENBURG
# ABOUT THE ZACK FILES:

*From a mother in New York, NY*: "Just wanted to let you know that it was THE ZACK FILES that made my son discover the joy of reading...I tried everything to get him interested...THE ZACK FILES turned my son into a reader overnight. Now he complains when he's out of books!"

*From a boy named Toby in New York, NY*: "The reason why I like your books is because you explain things that no other writer would even dream of explaining to kids."

*From Tara in Floral Park, NY*: "When I read your books I felt like I was in the book with you. We love your books!"

*From a teacher in West Chester, PA*: "I cannot thank you enough for writing such a fantastic series."

*From Max in Old Bridge, NJ*: "I wasn't such a great reader until I discovered your books."

*From Monica in Burbank, IL*: "I read almost all of your books and I loved the ones I read. I'm a big fan! *I'm Out of My Body, Please Leave a Message*. That's a funny title. It makes me think of it being the best book in the world."

*From three mothers in Toronto*: "You have managed to take three boys and unlock the world of reading. In January they could best be characterized as boys who 'read only under duress.' Now these same guys are similar in that they are motivated to READ."

*From Stephanie in Hastings, NY*: "If someone didn't like your books that would be crazy."

*From Dana in Floral Park, NY*: "I really LOVE I mean LOVE your books. I read them a million times. I wish I could buy more. They are so good and so funny."

*From a teacher in Pelham, NH*: "My students are thoroughly enjoying [THE ZACK FILES]. Some are reading a book a night."

*From Madeleine in Hastings, NY*: "I love your books...I hope you keep making many more Zack Files."

# THE ZACK FILES™

## Don't Count on Dracula

By Dan Greenburg

Illustrated by Jack E. Davis

GROSSET & DUNLAP • NEW YORK

For Judith, and for the real Zack,
with love—D.G.

I'd like to thank my editor
Jane O'Connor, who makes the process
of writing and revising so much fun,
and without whom
these books would not exist.

I also want to thank Jill Jarnow,
Emily Sollinger, and Tui Sutherland
for their terrific ideas.

Text copyright © 2000 by Dan Greenburg. Illustrations copyright © 2000 by Jack E. Davis.
All rights reserved. Published by Grosset & Dunlap, a division of Penguin Putnam Books
for Young Readers, New York. GROSSET & DUNLAP and THE ZACK FILES are trademarks
of Penguin Putnam Inc. Published simultaneously in Canada. Printed in the U.S.A.

*Library of Congress Cataloging-in-Publication Data is available.*

Greenburg, Dan
    Don't count on Dracula / by Dan Greenburg ; illustrated by Jack E. Davis.
        p. cm. — (The Zack files ; 21)
        Summary: Ten-year-old Zack gets a chance to meet the old horror film star
    Count Bugosi, who may or may not be a real vampire.
        [1. Vampires—Fiction. 2. Horror stories.] I. Davis, Jack E., ill. II. Title.
    PZ7.G8278 Do 2000
    [Fic]—dc21                                                              00-049050

ISBN  0-448-42175-5                    H I J

# Chapter 1

Who would you rather meet, a movie star or a vampire? Meeting either one would be so cool, I could never choose. Luckily, I didn't have to. I met both the same night.

Before I tell you about that, I should say who I am and stuff. My name is Zack. I'm ten and a half and I go to the Horace Hyde-White School for Boys in New York City. My parents are divorced, and I mostly live with my dad. The things that happen to me are probably a lot weirder than those that happen to you. Unless you've run into

Bigfoot at summer camp, or started turning into a cat, or watched your grandma become a teenager.

The thing I want to tell you about started at the opening of a new horror movie at a theater in Times Square. It was on a Friday. The movie was *Dracula Sucks*. It starred this real old European horror movie actor named Mella Bugosi as Count Dracula, the vampire. You might remember him from some of his other movies, like *Bats in the Belfry*, *Don't Count on Dracula*, *Coffin Medicine*, and *Fangs for Everything*.

Spencer and I love horror movies, and I have always been a big fan of Mella Bugosi. One of my favorite parts of a Mella Bugosi movie was when he fought a mummy at the end of *Mummy Dearest*.

Anyway, the opening was a pretty big deal. They had searchlights and crowds of people and camera crews from the local TV stations. Mella Bugosi was coming in from Transylvania, or wherever he hangs out.

Everybody who came to the opening was supposed to wear a costume. There were going to be prizes for the best ones. First prize was dinner with Mella Bugosi himself. I figured we didn't have any chance of winning, but it turned out not too many people wore costumes. Probably they were embarrassed or something.

Spencer and I decided to go as bags of blood, the kind they always have in the E.R. on hospital TV shows. We wore these big plastic bags, with places for our heads, arms, and legs to stick out. The bags were painted red. In big letters on the tops of the bags, we had our blood types. Spencer's blood is Type O. Mine is Type A Double Positive, which Dad says is really rare.

Ushers led us past velvet ropes into the

front of the theater. We marched up onstage before the movie began. The audience applauded for the costumes they liked best. Three judges would decide who got the most applause. One was Mella Bugosi. He wore a tuxedo and a cape, just like in his movies. His hair was white, but he looked pretty perky for an old guy.

"I heard Bugosi is really a vampire," I whispered to Spencer.

"Zack," said Spencer, "there's no such thing as vampires."

"How can you be so sure?" I asked.

"Because," said Spencer, "I've read up on it and I know." Spencer is probably the smartest kid in the whole state of New York. So if you disagree with him, you'd better have some pretty good proof.

The audience really liked the costumes that Spencer and I wore. They clapped and shouted for both of us. The judges gave us first prize! We were going to have dinner after the show with Mella Bugosi!

Then came the movie, *Dracula Sucks*. It was good, even though it was a lot like other Mella Bugosi movies. After the movie we went back to Dad's apartment to change out of our costumes. We were pretty excited about winning the dinner with Mella Bugosi. When we told Dad about our dinner, he was pretty excited, too.

"How the heck can you go to dinner with Mella Bugosi tonight?" he said. "Grandma Leah is coming in from Chicago."

"Well, maybe you could pick up Grandma at the airport. And then you could come back and get us at Mella Bugosi's hotel," I said. "We'll definitely be finished by then."

Dad sighed, which meant he was going to let me go. From somewhere we heard a distant rumble of thunder.

Dad dropped us off in front of the hotel.

"I'll be back in two hours to pick you up," said Dad. "Assuming the rain doesn't slow me down."

Spencer and I entered the hotel. We went up in the elevator and knocked on Bugosi's door. A butler guy opened it.

"Please?" said the butler. He had a funny accent.

"We're Zack and Spencer," I said. "The winners of the costume contest."

"One moment, please," said the butler.

He disappeared. About a minute later, Mr. Bugosi came to the door.

I couldn't believe we were standing face-to-face with the famous Mella Bugosi himself! This man was a movie star. At first I had trouble talking.

"H-how do you do, sir?" I said. "R-remember us? The winners of the c-costume

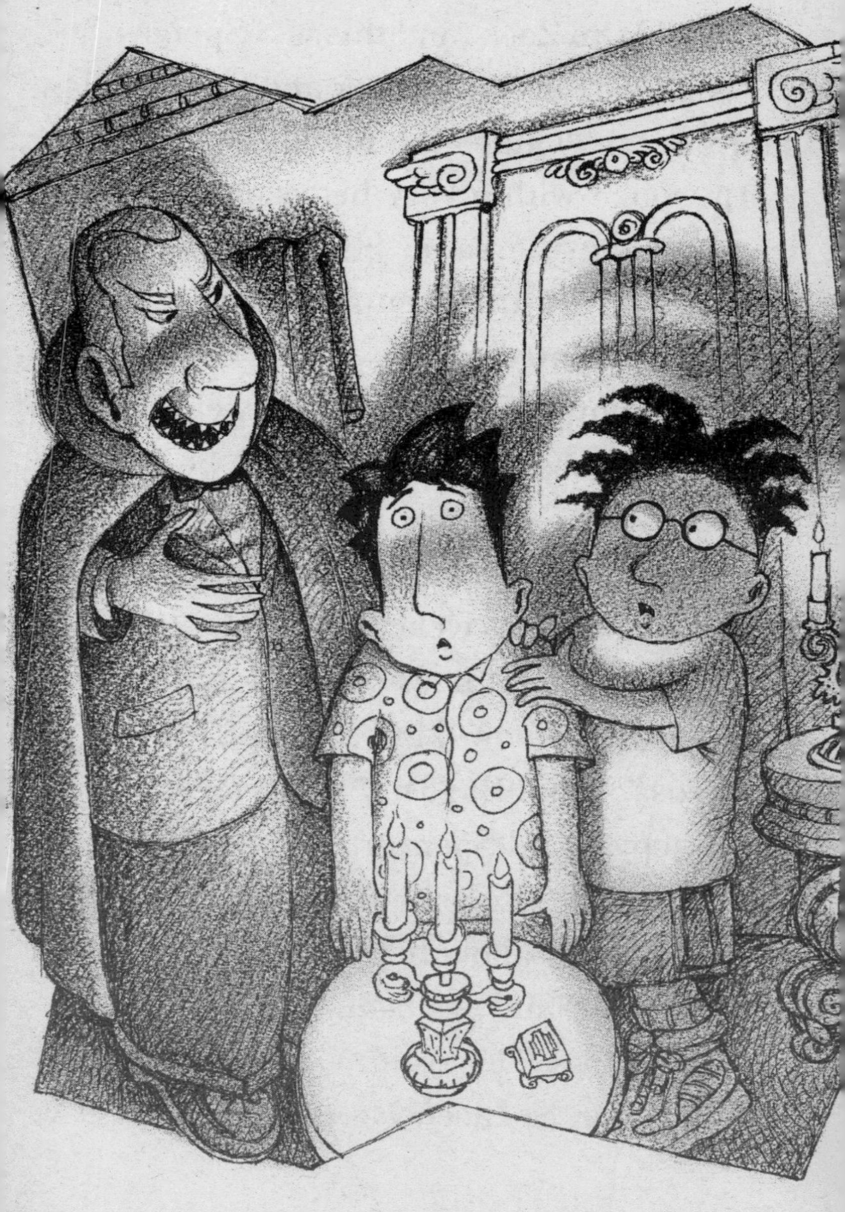

c-contest? I'm Zack, and this is S-Spencer."

"Ah. Gude evening, Zock and Spender," said Bugosi. "Gude evening."

He spoke with a very heavy accent. He was wearing the same black tuxedo and cape he wore at the opening. He seemed a little disappointed.

"I thought you were going to wear your waunderful costumes to dinner," he said. "I *lauve* your costumes. I *lauve* them."

"Thank you," I said. "But they were too uncomfortable to wear for dinner. Plus which, we thought bags of blood at dinner might be, you know, kind of gross."

"Gross?" said Bugosi. "What means?"

"Creepy," said Spencer.

"Creepy?" Bugosi repeated. "What could be creepy about bags of *blaud?* Blaud ees *lauvely*. Blaud ees *beautiful,* no?"

"Uh, yeah, OK," I said.

I looked at Spencer. He rolled his eyes.

The thunder rumbled again in the distance.

Then the butler waved us into Bugosi's hotel suite. There were black draperies over all the windows. The walls were painted black. There were black carpets on the floors. Just about everything in the suite was black. Maybe they developed film here. There were black candles all over the place. The only light came from the candles. The mirror above the fireplace was covered up with a black cloth.

"Look at that mirror," I whispered to Spencer. Vampires don't show up in mirrors, in case you didn't know.

"Bugosi is *not* a vampire," Spencer whispered back.

Bugosi took each of us by an elbow and led us into the living room.

"So," I said, "it's really an honor for us to be here, Mr. Bugosi."

"Eet ees *Count* Bugosi," he corrected me. "But that ees not eemportant. You may call me 'Your Excellency.' And eet ees *I* who am honored by *your* presence. Never have I seen sauch lauvely costumes."

"Thank you, Your Excellency," I said.

Bugosi nodded. The butler came into the living room.

"Would the young gentlemen like a dreenk before dinner?" he asked.

"Sure," I said. "Can I get a Dr. Pepper?"

Count Bugosi frowned.

"You weesh to see a doctor, Zock?" he said worriedly. "You are feeling seeck?"

"No, no, I'm fine," I said.

"Then why do you weesh Dr. Pooper?"

"Dr. *Pepper*," Spencer corrected him. "Not Pooper, *Pepper*. It's a drink."

"Ah, a *dreenk*," said the Count. He turned to the butler. "Pavlov, do we have sauch a dreenk by the name Dr. Pooper?"

"*Pepper.* No, Your Excellency."

"Ah," said the Count. "That saucks."

Outside, it began to rain. I heard raindrops patter against the windowpanes.

We went into the dining room for dinner. As soon as I sat down, I realized I had to go to the bathroom.

"Your Excellency, can you tell me where to find the, uh—the john?" I asked.

The Count frowned.

"You weesh to visit a person by the name of John?" he asked. "Why do you not wait until after dinner, Zock?"

"Oh, john isn't a person," I said.

"Ah," said Bugosi. "John ees dreenk?"

"No," I said. "In this country we sometimes call the *toilet* the john. I want to go to the *toilet*. Do you have a *toilet* here?"

"Of *course* we have toilet here, Zock. Do you theenk we do our business under the table?" The Count started laughing that creepy *har-har-har* laugh of his. "The toilet ees down the hall and to the right."

"Thanks, Your Excellency," I said.

I went down the hall and turned right. I had to go through the bedroom to get to the bathroom. Hmm. Right opposite the bed was a mini-bar. I love mini-bars. I wondered if there could be any Dr. Peppers in there. I opened the door and looked inside.

No candy. Just twenty cans of tomato juice, labeled "Type B Positive" and "Type A Negative." Yikes! This was not tomato juice. I was staring at twenty cans of blood! Was Count Bugosi a real vampire? If so, what were Spencer and I doing trapped in his hotel suite? And how could we get out of there before he decided to take a bite out of us?

# Chapter 2

I had to get a hold of myself. I had to calm down. I went into the bathroom. The toilet was black, too. I took a deep breath.

Mella Bugosi wasn't a vampire, I told myself. He was an old horror film star who played the *part* of a vampire in his movies. And the juice labeled with blood types in his mini-bar was just part of the act.

Yeah. For a minute there, I almost let my imagination get the best of me. Whew! I felt a lot calmer by the time I got back to the dinner table and Spencer.

The rain outside was getting fierce. A sudden crash of thunder made me jump.

"So, Zock," said Count Bugosi, "you find your friend John?"

"Yeah," I said. In front of my plate was water in a delicate old glass goblet. I reached for it. But the glass slipped out of my hand. It shattered into about a million pieces.

"I'm so sorry, Your Excellency!" I said.

I started picking up the pieces, and one of them cut my hand. A little drop of blood got on the white tablecloth.

"Uh-oh," I said. "I got my Type A Double Positive on your tablecloth."

Count Bugosi's eyes almost popped right out of his head.

"You have Type A Dooble Positive?" he squeaked. He leaned across the table and grabbed my hand. His eyes were kind of wild-looking.

"Best theeng to do weeth a cut," he said hoarsely, "ees sauck the wound."

He raised my hand to his lips. I pulled my hand away.

"Uh, that's OK, Your Excellency," I said. "It's just a tiny cut."

"Ees what they say in first-aid books," said the Count. "Sauck the wound!"

"That's only for snakebites," said Spencer. "You suck the wound to get out the venom. There isn't any venom here."

The Count reached for my hand again.

"What the heck," he said. "I sauck it anyway."

"No, thanks," I said, pulling my hand away again. "I'm OK."

"No, no," said the Count. "We must sauck the wound. Ees what *doctors* recommend. Ees what *hospitals* recommend. Ees what the surgeon general heemself recommend. Sauck the wound!"

"Maybe later," I said. I don't know why I said that. I didn't want anybody—not even somebody famous—sucking on my hand. I guess I'm just too polite for my own good.

I got up and started toward the bathroom.

"I'll come with you," said Spencer.

I could tell he was scared to stay in the room alone with Count Bugosi.

In the bathroom medicine cabinet we found some Band-Aids.

"So, what do you think, Spencer?" I whispered. "You still think there's no such thing as a vampire?"

"There has never been any proof of such a thing," said Spencer.

"Then what about all that 'sauck the wound' business?"

"I don't know. Maybe he's just trying to be helpful. You know, saliva is an anti-septic, the same as hydrogen peroxide."

"Yeah, right," I said. "You know what I found in the mini-bar on my last trip to the john? Blood!"

"Get out of here," said Spencer.

"You think I'm kidding?" I said.

I led him out of the john, into the bedroom. I opened the mini-bar.

"OK, Spencer, what do you see?"

"Tomato juice?" asked Spencer hopefully.

"No tomato juice is labeled 'Type A Negative' or 'Type B Positive,'" I said.

"Look," he said. "We shouldn't jump to crazy conclusions. There could be a perfectly logical explanation for this."

Then we both saw it. At the foot of the bed was a carved wooden chest six feet long.

"Oh, no," I said. "Could that be what I think it is? A coffin!"

"I'm sure it's just a wooden chest to hold blankets," said Spencer.

"I dare you to open it," I said.

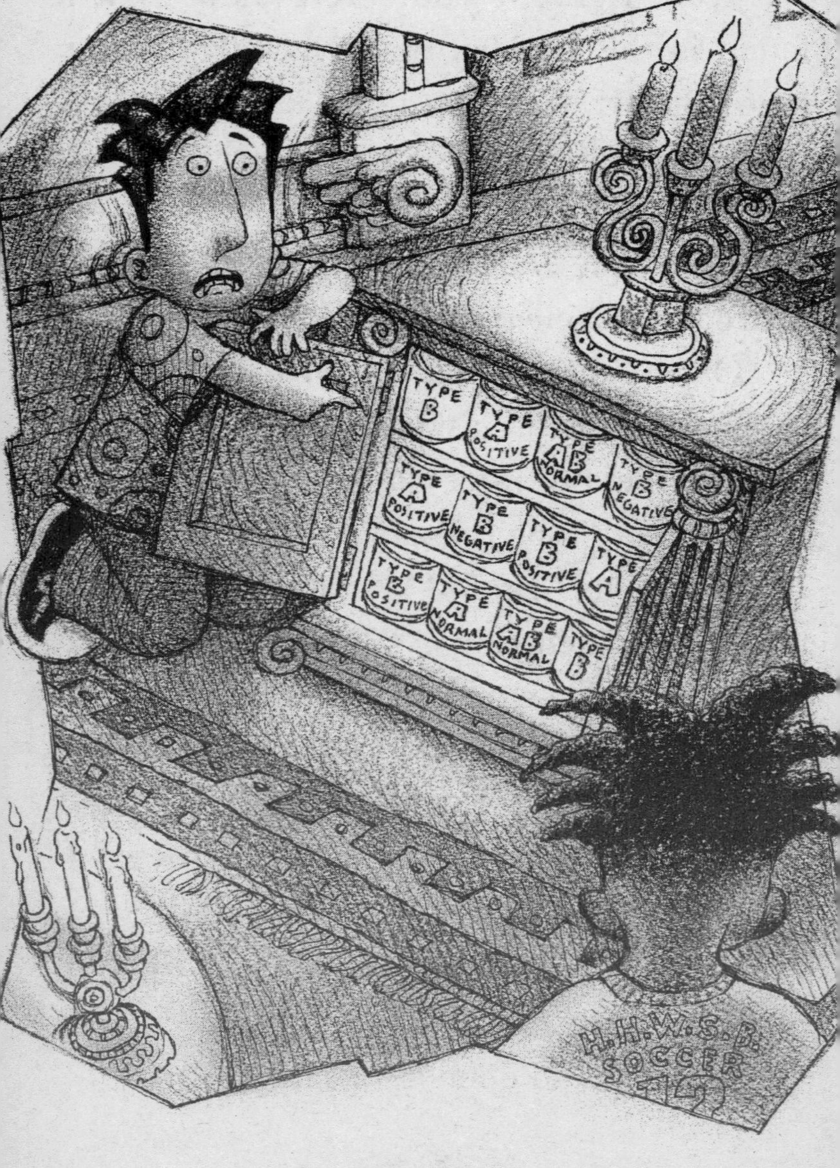
TYPE B
TYPE A POSITIVE
TYPE AB NORMAL
TYPE A POSITIVE
TYPE B NEGATIVE
TYPE B POSITIVE
TYPE B NEGATIVE
TYPE B POSITIVE
TYPE A NORMAL
TYPE AB NORMAL
TYPE A
TYPE B
H.H.W.S.B.
SOCCER

"You *dare* me? Why don't you *bet* me?"

"OK," I said. "You're on. I'll bet you a buck you don't have the guts to open that coffin."

"And *I'll* bet *you* it's not a coffin."

"How much?"

"Five bucks."

"You're on!"

We shook hands. Then we inched closer to the carved wooden chest.

"Go ahead," I said. "Open it."

"OK," said Spencer. He reached down and opened the chest. At that exact moment, the loudest clap of thunder I ever heard split the air.

We both screamed. But it wasn't because of the thunder. It was because of what we saw inside the wooden chest.

# Chapter 3

The carved wooden chest was lined with black quilted satin. It was definitely a coffin. Inside it was a made-up bed with blankets, sheets and a pillow. There was a little plush bat toy on the blankets. The sheets had been turned down for the night. There were little foil-wrapped chocolates on the pillow.

"Oh boy," I whispered. "He really *is* a vampire."

"There must be some other explanation," said Spencer.

"Like what?" I asked. "You think he's

just a normal guy who likes to sleep in coffins?"

"I don't know. But I just can't believe in vampires."

"What would it take to convince you, Spencer? Having him bite you on the neck and suck out all your blood? By the way, you owe me five dollars."

"Four," said Spencer. "You owe me a dollar for opening it."

"Never mind that now," I said. "We've got to get out of here. Fast."

I closed the coffin lid and turned around. Count Bugosi was standing there, staring at us. I had no idea how long he'd been standing there. I didn't know if he saw us looking in his coffin or what.

"Oh, uh, hi there, Your Excellency," I said. "How's it going? Some storm outside there, huh? Well, we can certainly use the rainfall. Especially the farmers. And the reservoirs are at their lowest level in years, yes sir." I was so nervous I was babbling now, but I didn't care.

"What you are doing een my badroom?" asked the Count.

"In your *bad*room? Oh, your *bed*room. Is this your bedroom? I didn't realize it was your bedroom. Nice bedroom. Nice, uh, bed. Nice...room." I looked at my watch. "Oh, wow, is it that late already? I had no idea it was that late. I'm afraid we have to leave. Hate to cut my hand and run, but we have another appointment and we're really really late."

I grabbed Spencer and pulled him toward the door. Thunder exploded just outside the bedroom window.

"What other appointment?" asked the Count. He looked really upset.

"What other appointment?" I said. "An

appointment for, uh, dinner. That's right. Spencer and I won another dinner with another movie star at another opening we went to yesterday. So we really have to go. But we had a great time, no kidding. We'll have to do it again sometime when we're not so rushed."

"Maybe tomorrow?" said the Count.

"Maybe tomorrow?" I said. "OK, sure." I would have agreed to anything at that point, just to get us out of there.

Ahead of us was a door. I yanked it open and pulled Spencer after me. We hadn't gotten out of the Count's hotel suite. We'd walked into a linen closet. We backed out.

"Just wanted to be sure you've got enough towels before we left. You're fine," I said. I found the right door and practically pulled Spencer's arm off getting him out of there.

# Chapter 4

By the time Spencer and I got home, Dad and Grandma were kind of upset.

"Look at them," said Grandma Leah, giving me a big hug. "Soaked to the skin. I hope you don't catch pneumonia."

My grandma is in her eighties, but you'd never know it. She's got more pep than most kids my age. And she spends most of her time worrying that everybody isn't warm enough or dry enough or something.

"Why didn't you wait for us to pick you up at the hotel?" Dad asked.

"We had to get out of there fast," I said. "Mella Bugosi is a vampire!"

"Well, we're not positive about that yet," said Spencer. "But he's really creepy."

"Mella Bugosi?" said Grandma Leah. "Many years ago there was a movie actor by that name. This one must be his son."

"No, it's the same guy, Grandma," I said. "And he's a vampire."

"Yes, yes, I remember now," said Grandma Leah. "He played a vampire in the movies. Grandpa Sam and I saw a few of them. He was very enjoyable to watch. Is this the man you had dinner with?"

"Yes," I said. "And he's a vampire."

"In the *movies* he was a vampire," said Grandma Leah.

"In the movies *and* in real life," I said.

"Zack, this is nonsense."

"But we have *proof* he's a vampire. Tell them, Spencer."

We all looked at Spencer.

"This Bugosi is a pretty weird guy," said Spencer. "In his mini-bar we saw tomato juice marked 'Type A Negative' and 'Type B Positive.' Of course, that doesn't necessarily prove it's blood."

"Tell them about the coffin," I said.

"He's got a carved wooden chest that looks just like a coffin," said Spencer.

"*Looks* like a coffin? It *is* a coffin," I said. "He sleeps in it!"

"Well, we don't know that he sleeps in it," said Spencer. "I mean, we didn't *see* him sleeping in it."

"OK, then what about wanting to suck the cut I got?" I asked.

"Who wanted to do that?" Dad asked.

"What cut?" asked Grandma, alarmed. "Did somebody cut you? Who cut you?"

"Relax, Grandma, it's no big deal."

About the worst thing you can do

around my grandma is to say there's anything wrong with you. It was all Dad and Spencer and I could do to keep her from dragging me off to the hospital.

"If you won't go to the hospital," said Grandma, "then you must go to bed immediately. Loss of blood makes the body weak. You don't want to faint, do you?"

I groaned. I protested. After a while I just went to bed. It was easier than arguing with Grandma Leah.

By the next morning, Saturday, the rain had stopped. Although it was still gloomy out, Grandma wanted to go sightseeing. We walked down Fifth Avenue, window shopping. Then I talked Grandma into going to the Bronx Zoo. They had a new exhibit on bats that our science teacher had told us about. It sounded pretty cool.

So, an hour later, we were in a big dark room, standing behind a huge pane of glass. On the other side was a bat cave. When your eyes got accustomed to the gloom, you could see dozens and dozens of bats—swooping and flapping and fluttering all over the place. Some were hanging upside down from the roof of the cave. It *was* cool. It was also kind of creepy.

"Zock!" said a voice. "How pleasant to see you!"

My heart froze. It was the Count!

"How pleasant to see you, Zock," said the Count again. "And who ees thees lauvely young lady?"

"Oh, hi, Your Excellency," I said. "This is my Grandma Leah. Grandma Leah, this is Count Mella Bugosi. We can't stop to talk. We have an appointment."

"Another appointment," said the Count. "You certainly are a beezy boy." Then he turned to my grandma and bowed.

"I am so happy to meet you, Count

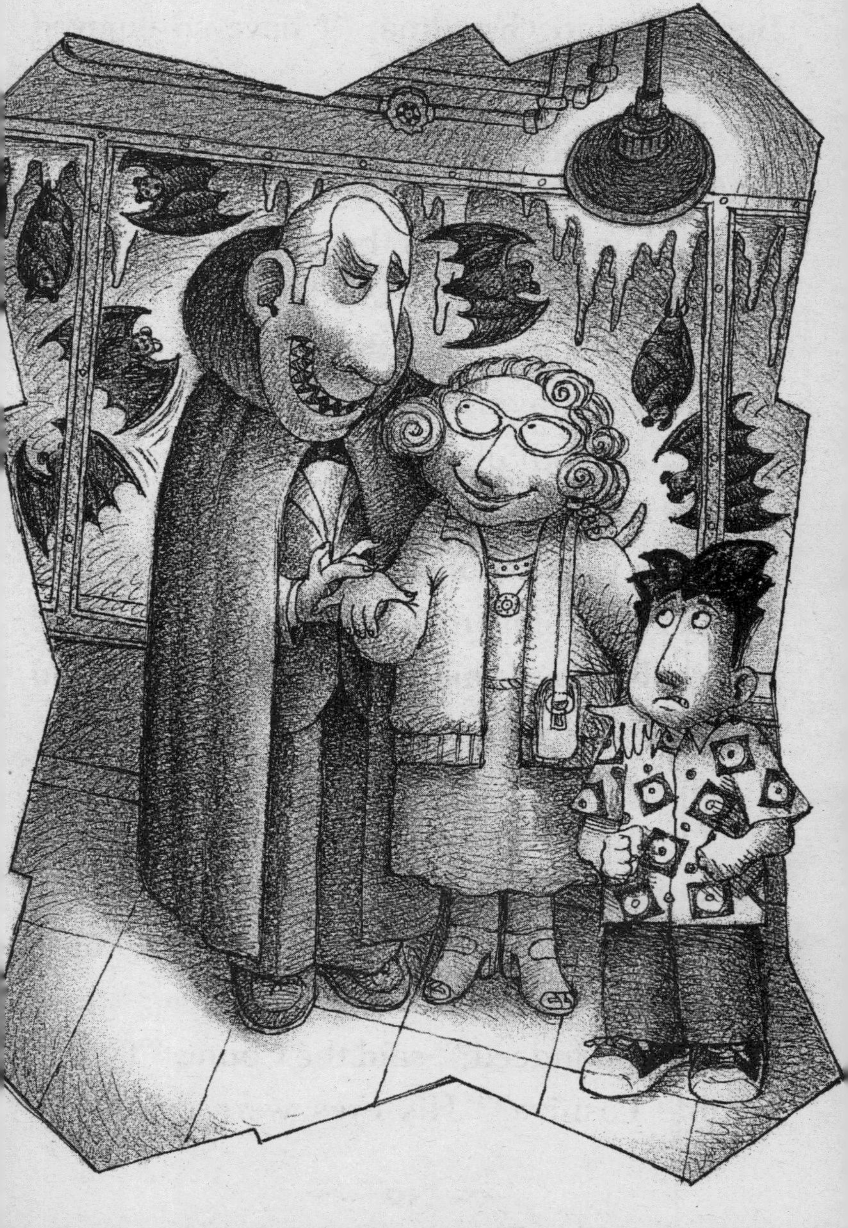

Bugosi," said Grandma. "I have so enjoyed your films."

The Count's cape swept the floor as he made another deep bow and kissed Grandma Leah's hand. Even in the darkened room I could tell that she was blushing.

"Your beauty," said the Count, "eet takes my breath away from eenside of my lungs. I suffocate weeth pleasure."

"Zack was telling us what a nice time he had with you last night," said Grandma.

"Eet ees unfortunate that he cut hees hand and rush away," said the Count. "The wound keeped on bleeding and bleeding."

I swear he was practically licking his lips.

"Oh, that's because he has this rare blood type," said Grandma. "Type A Double Positive. It doesn't clot as fast as the others. I have the same thing myself."

"Do you indeed?" said the Count. "Type A Dooble Positive?" His eyes were sparkling.

"How eenteresting! And why do you call Zock your grandson? Surely you are not old enough to be even hees *mauther*."

Grandma giggled. I don't remember ever hearing Grandma giggle before.

"Count Bugosi," said Grandma, "I am certainly old enough to be Zack's grandmother. I'm eighty-eight years old."

"Never have I met a lady as beautiful as you, my dear Leah," said the Count. "And I have known the beegest stars een Hollywood and Europe. The beegest!"

Oh, boy. The Count was laying it on pretty thick. But Grandma didn't seem to mind at all. That made me really nervous.

"C'mon, Grandma," I said. "We'd better hurry or we'll be late."

"Late for what?" she asked.

"That thing we were going to do," I said.

"I don't remember," she said.

"Madame Leah," said the Count,

"porhops you weel do me the honor to dine weeth me tonight? I must take you to a waunderful Transylvanian restaurant I know."

"Whoops!" I said. "Can't do that either, Your Excellency. We're busy tonight, too. Grandma, remember that thing we promised we'd do with Dad?"

"What thing was that?" asked Grandma.

"That, uh...*opera* I wanted to see so badly." This was a joke, of course. I can't stand operas. But I thought it sounded impressive enough for the Count.

"Zack, dear," said Grandma, "I don't remember any plans we had to go to the opera. But I'm sure your father won't mind if the two of you go by yourselves. Tonight I'd really like to dine with Count Bugosi."

"Dear lady, I am speechless weeth happiness," said the Count. "I shall peeck you up at eight o'clock p.m."

"Then let me give you our address," said Grandma. She wrote down our address, and gave it to him.

"Eight o'clock," said the Count. "I weel be counting the hours and the minutes."

Count Bugosi bowed deeply for the third time, kissed Grandma's hand again, and disappeared in the gloom of the bat exhibit.

"What a lovely man," said Grandma.

"Grandma," I said, grabbing her by the elbows. "You can't go out to dinner with him!"

"Why not, dear?" said Grandma.

"Didn't you hear what I told you last night? The man is a vampire! He likes you because of your blood type!"

"Zack, don't talk nonsense. Come, we must go home right away. I need to get to a hairdresser and have my hair done for my dinner tonight. Just think...I'm eighty-eight and I'm going on a date with a movie star!"

# Chapter 5

"So, where is she now?" asked Spencer.

"Having her hair done," I said. "Getting ready for her big date with the vampire."

We were in Spencer's room, working at his computer. As soon as I left Grandma I'd called Spencer and told him I had to come over. We were looking up vampires on the Internet. I hoped I could find something to stop Mella Bugosi from biting my grandma, but the only vampire stuff we'd found so far was about little brown bats that lived in South America.

"You know, Zack, we could be wrong," said Spencer. "I still don't see why you're so sure he's a vampire." He was scrolling through a section on fruit bats.

"Are you kidding me?" I said. "*You* were in his hotel suite. *You* saw the cans of blood in the mini-bar and the coffin in his bedroom. *You* saw how hot he was to suck my bloody hand."

"Look," said Spencer, "I admit the guy's a weirdo. But there are lots of weirdos in New York. That doesn't make them vampires. Besides, he's taking your grandmother to a restaurant. I'm sure she'll be safe in a public place. Hey, here's something. A list of things to stop vampires."

"Let me see that," I said. I looked where he was pointing. "Hmmm...a necklace of garlic...holding up a crucifix...driving a wooden stake through the heart... Personally, I don't have the guts to even *criticize* somebody, so I doubt I could drive a wooden stake through his heart. And as for garlic and crucifixes, well, that stuff has been around so long, I'm sure that any vampire knows how to get around it."

"Well, excuse *me*," said Spencer.

"I'm sorry," I said. "I know you're trying to help. What we need is somebody who knows about stuff that wouldn't be on any website. Somebody like—"

"Mrs. Coleman-Levin," said Spencer.

"Exactly," I said.

Besides being our teacher, Mrs. Coleman-Levin knows a lot about weird stuff. She's pretty weird herself. She has a jar on her desk with a pig's brain in it. She has a real human skeleton standing up in the corner. She keeps a piranha in a tank in our homeroom and feeds it live goldfish. She works at the morgue on weekends, cutting up bodies to see what they died of.

"You think Mrs. Coleman-Levin would mind if we went over to her place now and bugged her about vampires?" I asked.

"Probably," said Spencer. "But that has never stopped us before."

"Good point," I said.

When she opened the door, Mrs. Coleman-Levin was wearing some weird kind of robe. It was kind of silvery. I can't be absolutely positive of this, but as the door was swinging open I could swear she was floating a couple of inches off the floor.

"Good afternoon, boys," she said. "Come on in. I had a feeling I might be seeing you right about now."

"Honest?" I said. "Did you see that in a vision, or what?"

"Actually, no," she said. "Spencer phoned me right before you left his house. Now, what may I do for you?"

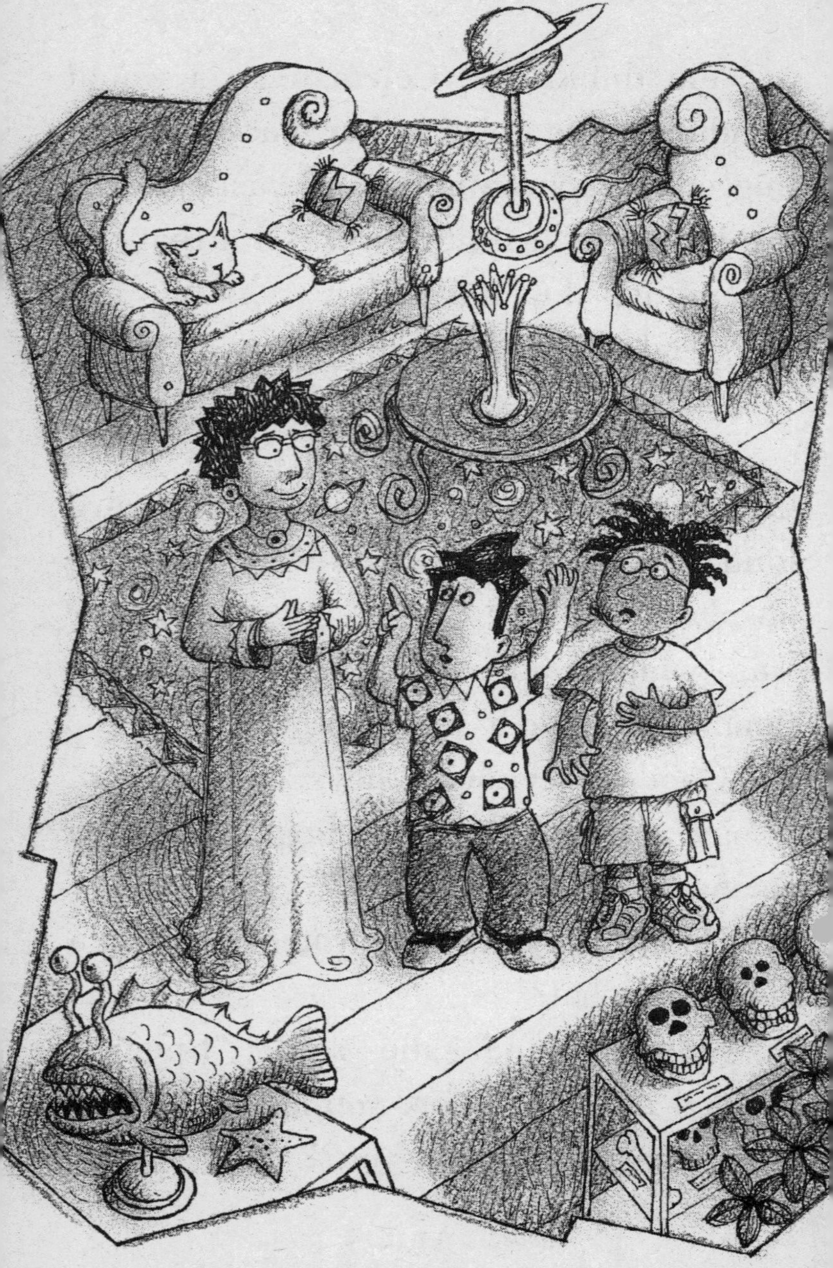

"Mrs. Coleman-Levin, how do you stop a vampire?"

She thought this over a moment, frowning. Then she shrugged and smiled.

"I give up," she said. "How do you stop a vampire?"

"You don't know?" said Spencer.

"I didn't say I didn't know. I thought you were asking me a riddle."

"It's not a riddle," I said. "It's a real live problem. My Grandma Leah is having dinner with a real vampire tonight at eight o'clock. She has this gourmet blood type—so do I. And I'm scared he's going to have a few cocktails of it unless we can find some way to stop him."

"Whoa," said Mrs. Coleman-Levin. "Slow down. Who's this vampire, and why's your grandma going to dinner with him?"

"OK," I said. "The vampire is Mella Bugosi..."

"The old horror film actor?" said Mrs Coleman-Levin. "I *love* him! I've seen all o his movies. He was great in *Bats in the Belfry* And *Fangs for Everything*."

"Mrs. Coleman-Levin, we don't have much time. Spencer and I were invited to dinner a Mella Bugosi's hotel. We found cans of blood in his mini-bar, and a coffin in his bedroom He met my grandma this afternoon at the zoo, and he invited her to dinner."

"I see," said Mrs. Coleman-Levin.

"Zack and I tried to look up things on the Internet about stopping vampires," said Spencer. "But all we came up with was..."

"...garlic, crucifixes, and stakes through the heart," she said. "Those *are* the standard ways to stop a vampire."

"Do you know anything better?" I asked.

"Perhaps," said Mrs. Coleman-Levin "One could become invisible. Sometimes that works."

"Isn't there anything else you could suggest?"

Mrs. Coleman-Levin smiled a strange smile. Without saying a word, she walked out of the room. I looked at Spencer. When she came back in, she was carrying a clear plastic Ziploc freezer bag filled with something that looked like dumplings or Chinese eggrolls.

"What's that?" I asked.

"Knishes," she answered. "Vampires hate them."

"What's a knish?" asked Spencer.

"I know all about knishes," I said. "My grandma makes them. They weigh about five pounds each and give you gas for two days. Why would vampires hate them?"

"Vampires don't hate *all* knishes," said Mrs. Coleman-Levin. "But these knishes are filled with wolfsbane, mandrake root, garlic, and chopped liver. Quite tasty, really.

But they seem to have a particularly bad effect on vampires. I've never been able to figure out why. Whatever it is, the combination is really upsetting to them."

"If vampires hate knishes so much," I said, "then how are we supposed to get Count Bugosi to eat one?"

"Oh, he doesn't have to *eat* a knish to have it work," said Mrs. Coleman-Levin. "I should think that merely holding it up in front of him will do the trick."

"And what if it *doesn't* do the trick?"

"Oh, in that case," said Mrs. Coleman-Levin with a grin, "he'll probably suck your blood and you'll all be sleeping in coffins for the rest of time." She handed me the bag of knishes. "Do let me know how it all turns out. Good luck!"

# Chapter 6

We left Mrs. Coleman-Levin's at around 6:30 P.M. By the time we got back to my Dad's apartment it was almost 7:00. I still had an hour left to try to talk Grandma out of going to dinner with the Count before he picked her up at 8:00. If that didn't work, we'd have to go to the restaurant with the knishes.

My dad was in the kitchen. Four pots were bubbling on the stove, and cooking stuff was scattered all over the place.

"Hi, Zack. Hi, Spencer," said Dad.

"Hey, what do you guys have in the bag?"

"Vampire knishes," I said.

"I wish you'd told me you were bringing home takeout," said Dad. "I'm making a special dinner for us. Meatball lasagna."

"Oh, this isn't for us to eat," I said. "It's for scaring off vampires. Is Grandma getting dressed, or what?"

"No," said Dad. "Grandma's already left."

"What?"

"There was a change in plan. Mr. Bugosi picked her up early."

"Uh-oh. What time did he pick her up?"

"Oh, gosh. About an hour ago. Why?"

"Dad, do you know the name of the restaurant they went to? This is really important. It's some kind of Transylvanian place, I think."

"I don't think they went to a restaurant," said Dad. "They were going to a party at the home of some friends of his. And then they were going back to his hotel to have dinner in his suite."

"Oh, no! This is terrible!" I said. "Dad, Grandma is in real danger! We have to go to the hotel and rescue her!"

"Zack, Grandma's a grown woman," said Dad. "She can take care of herself."

"Not with vampires, she can't!"

"Zack, Mr. Bugosi is a movie star. He's not a vampire."

I screamed and banged my head against the wall. Spencer and Dad looked like I'd gone bananas.

"Dad, why don't you ever *believe* me? You didn't believe that my orthodontist could turn into a monster until you saw it yourself! You didn't believe I was turning into a cat until I grew whiskers and pointy ears! You didn't believe I could read minds or that my cat could talk or that it was a poltergeist who was trashing our apartment! Why don't you ever *believe* me till it's too *late*!"

Dad sighed and shook his head.

"I'm sorry, Zack," he said. "You're absolutely right. The things you tell me are often unbelievable. But they do turn out to be true almost all the time."

*"Almost* all the time*?"* I screamed. *"Almost?* Tell me one time when what I said didn't turn out to be true. Tell me one time!"

"OK, calm down, Zack," said Dad. "I can't think of any."

"So if I tell you that Count Bugosi is a vampire...?"

"Then he probably sucks blood," said Dad. "So, what do you want me to do?"

"Come with me and Spencer to the Count's hotel to save Grandma," I said.

"All right," said Dad. "But my meatball lasagna is going to be ruined!"

# Chapter 7

At first Pavlov wasn't going to let us in.

"Ees not here, the Count," he said.

"I happen to know he's having dinner with my grandma in there," I said.

Dad pushed him aside and we burst into the suite. It was even darker than the last time. In the dining room sat Mella Bugosi and Grandma.

"Ah, gude evening," said the Count. "What a pleasant surprise." I could tell he wasn't too thrilled to see us.

"Zack! Dan! Spencer!" said my grandma.

"What are *you* doing here?"

"Rescuing you," I said. "Please, Grandma. Let's get out of here."

"I don't need rescuing," said Grandma. "Mella and I are having a perfectly lovely time. He took me to a party, a wonderful party." Her eyes were sparkling in a way I'd never seen before. "There were so many lovely people there, Zack. Movie stars. And Mella introduced me to all of them."

Dad turned to me. "Maybe this is the one time you're wrong," he said.

"I'm not wrong," I said. "And we're not leaving here without Grandma."

"Please," said the Count. "Seet down and stay. There ees plenty for everybody."

"Well," said Spencer, "I *am* kind of hungry. What do you have?"

"Anytheeng you weesh," said the Count. "Chocolate sundaes. Roast peeg. Bobble gum. French fries. Even Dr. Pooper."

"Well," said Dad, "I'm kind of hungry, too. Zack, maybe we *could* just have a bite to eat, and then Grandma will come home with us. Is that all right?"

I rolled my eyes. Why was I the only person taking this situation seriously?

"I guess so," I said.

"Waunderful!" said the Count. "Pavlov, please to pour some champagne for Madame Leah and her son. I have sometheeng eemportant to say."

"Yes, Your Excellency," said Pavlov.

Then Count Bugosi lifted his glass.

"Lady and gentlemens," he said, "I am so hoppy. Een all my years I have never met such a waunderful woman as Leah. I theenk I have fallen een lauve weeth her."

The Count dropped down to one knee.

"Een front of your family," said the Count, "I now ask: Weel you marry me, beautiful madame?"

Oh, boy. This was about the last thing in the world I expected. I looked at Grandma Leah. She was smiling in kind of a sad way. I thought I saw tears in her eyes.

I knew that she would say no. She's always said that when Grandpa Sam died, she never wanted to get married again.

"Dear Mella," said Grandma. "I do not know what to say. Can I think about your proposal for a while?"

My mouth fell open. I looked at Dad.

"Mom," said my dad, "what are you saying? Haven't you always told us you never wanted to get remarried? You only met this man a day ago. How could you even *think* about marrying him?"

"But Mella is so charming," said Grandma. "And we've been having such a wonderful time."

"Leah, dear," said the Count, "what ees your answer?"

"I...I need time to think," said Grandma.

"Time?" said the Count. "A man of seventy-five does not have that much time."

"You're seventy-five?" said Grandma. "I'm eighty-eight. You are much too young for me. If I married you, people would say I was robbing the cradle."

"All right," he said. "I am not seventy-five. I am *three hundred* and seventy-five."

"Aha!" I cried. "He's a vampire!"

"No!" shouted Pavlov. "Eet ees not true! The Count ees not a vampire!"

Bugosi held up his hands. He stood up.

"All right, all right," he said. "Yes, I admit eet. Eet ees true. I am a vampire."

"See?" I shouted. "What did I tell you!"

"So, I am a vampire," said the Count. "So what? Dear Leah, eef you marry me, I weel geeve you eternal life. You weel never grow old. We weel be together forever!"

Grandma Leah shook her head.

"I don't *want* to live forever," she said. She reached across the table and took the Count's hand. "Mella, I am honored by your wanting to marry me. But I cannot do so."

The Count's face got red and angry.

"*Nobody* turns down proposal of marriage from Count Bugosi!" he screamed. "*Nobody!*"

He turned toward me. His eyes were red and glowing. His teeth began growing longer before my very eyes.

"Eet ees all *your* fault that she does not weesh to marry me! *Your* fault! But I shall steel have some Dooble A Positive blaud!"

He lunged toward me.

"The knishes, Zack! The knishes!" screamed Spencer.

The Count punched Dad, grabbed me by the front of my shirt, and held on tight. Boy, was he strong!

"Mella! Stop this!" Grandma shouted.

I struggled with the bag of knishes that Mrs. Coleman-Levin had given us, trying to open it. But I was so panicky I had a hard time getting the Ziploc top to open. At last I grabbed one of the knishes out of the bag and shoved it in his face.

"A *knish*?" he shouted. "You theenk a *knish* weel save you now? I *spit* on your knish! Your knish means *nothing* to me! *Nothing*, do you hear? Here, I show you!"

The Count grabbed a knish and ate half in one bite. He seemed fine. Then suddenly he gasped and let go of me. He backed up several steps. I thought maybe he was having gas pains.

He began to shudder. And then, as Dad, Grandma, Spencer and I stared in fascination, he started growing smaller. Smaller and smaller, until he was only the size of a cat. He was now covered completely in fur. He unfolded long leathery wings. He was turning into a bat!

"Oh, no!" cried Pavlov. "Your Excellency! What has happened to you?"

Pavlov ran to the open window and tried to close it. But he wasn't fast enough. The bat flapped its wings and flew out the window into the New York night.

"Come back, Your Excellency!" Pavlov shouted.

Dad, Spencer, Pavlov, Grandma, and I stared at the open window, unable to speak. Finally, Dad turned to me.

"My gosh," he said. "I have never in my life seen anything so strange."

"Yes, you have, Dad," I said weakly. "Lots of times."

I turned to my grandma. She seemed kind of dazed.

"Grandma," I said, "are you all right?"

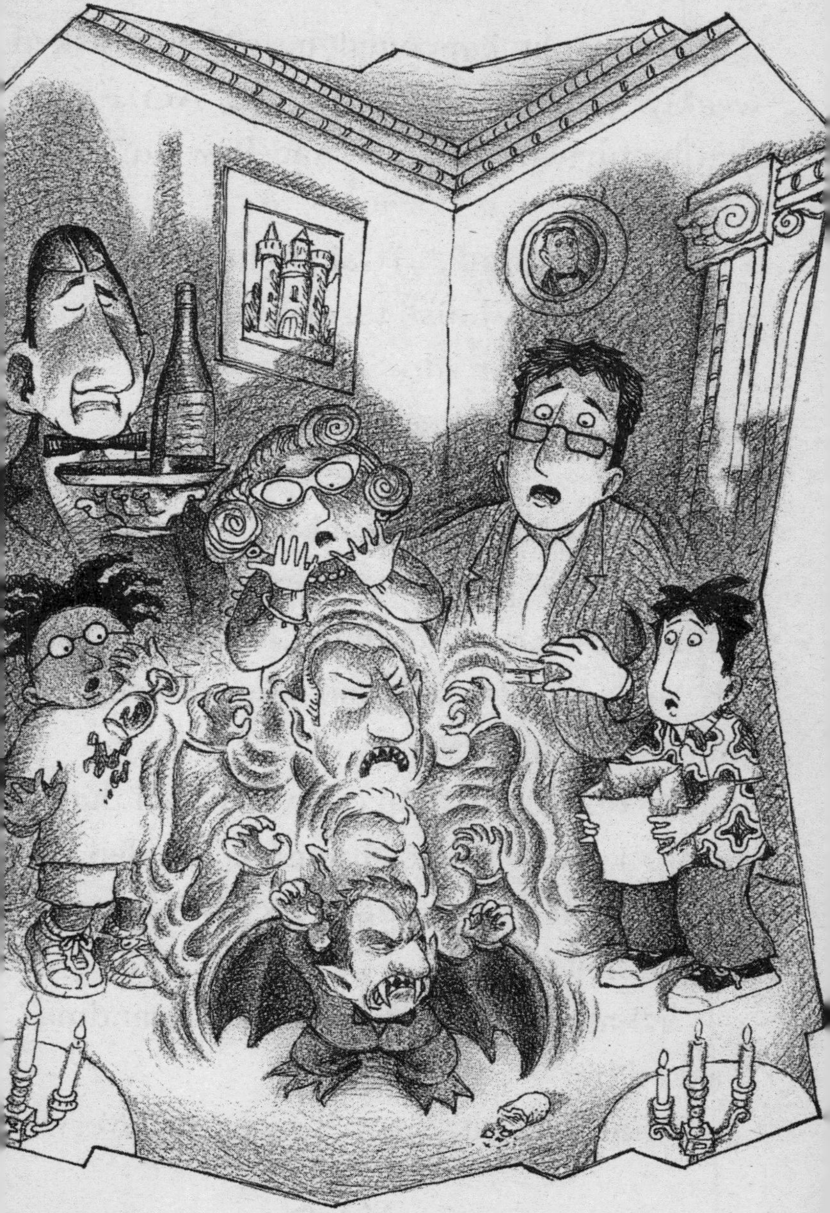

"What just happened here?" she asked weakly. "Where did Mella go? Am I right that he turned into a bat and flew out of the window?"

"Yes, Grandma," I said, "he was a vampire. I guess my knish turned him into a bat."

"Knishes can do such a thing?" said Grandma. "Who knew?"

───╱╲───

When we left the hotel suite, Pavlov was clutching the plush bat from the coffin and sobbing. After we got home, Dad tried to finish making his lasagna. But nobody had much of an appetite.

The rest of the weekend wasn't all that exciting. I don't think Grandma minded. But once, when she thought I couldn't hear, I caught her sighing.

"What are you sighing about, Grandma?" I asked her.

"Hearing a man say he was in love with

me was very pleasant," she answered. "I haven't heard a man say that to me in a very long time. He was a charming man. But it never would have worked. It would have been much too difficult being the wife of a bat."

~~~

I never heard a thing about the Count again. So after about a month, I threw out all the remaining vampire knishes.

Then yesterday, Mrs. Coleman-Levin took our science class to the Bronx Zoo. At the bat exhibit we all crowded into the gloomy room. All the guys pressed their noses against the glass, trying to see the bats as they flapped and swooped around their cave.

"Zock! Spender!" said a voice behind us. "What a pleasant surprise."

I turned around. It was the Count! Both Spencer and I backed away from him.

"Uh, h-how you doing?" I asked.

"Not so good," said the Count. "How ees the lovely Madame Leah?"

"She's fine," I said.

"Since she refuse to be my wife, I am in mourning," said the Count. "When you speak to her, tell her I geeve up my old ways. Tell her I am now a much deeferent man. Tell her next time she ees coming to New York, maybe we can have a dreenk."

"OK," I said.

"Tomato juice only," he said. "I geeve up the other stuff."

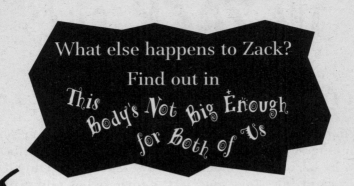

What else happens to Zack?

Find out in

*This Body's Not Big Enough for Both of Us*

"Ssshhh!" said Madam Poopah. "Sometimes it takes them a while to get through to us. It's quite difficult for the dead to communicate with the living."

Then I heard a weird high-pitched noise. It seemed to be coming from Madam Poopah.

Then something even weirder happened. I felt a kind of tingling from Madam Poopah's hand. Then something that felt like a slight electric shock.

Then I heard a ghostly voice.

**"Who dares to disturb the spirits of the dead?"** it said.

It was the voice of a very grouchy old lady. It had a strong British accent.

But the weirdest thing about the voice was...it was coming from *me!*

# THE ZACK FILES™

## OUT-OF-THIS-WORLD FAN CLUB!

Looking for even more info on all the strange, otherworldly
happenings going on in *The Zack Files*? Get the inside
scoop by becoming a member of *The Zack Files* Out-Of-This-
World Fan Club! Just send in the form below and we'll
send you your *Zack Files* Out-Of-This-World Fan Club kit in-
cluding an official fan club membership card, a really cool
*Zack Files* magnet, and a newsletter featuring excerpts from
Zack's upcoming paranormal adventures, supernatural news
from around the world, puzzles, and more! And as a member you'll continue to receive the newsletter six times a
year! The best part is—it's all free!

✄ -------------------------------------------------------------

☐ Yes! I want to check out *The Zack Files*
   Out-Of-This-World Fan Club!

name: _____ age: _____

address: _____

city/town: _____ state: ___ zip: _____

Send this form to:     Penguin Putnam Books for
                       Young Readers
                       Mass Merchandise Marketing
                       Dept. ZACK
                       345 Hudson Street
                       New York, NY 10014